Magic wasn't something I had to go in search of;
it was here, within me, all the time.
When hearts are open, when love is flowing, magic happens.

- Katrina Kenison

To Kenia & Bianca Jade, my inner glow.
My best self rises always for you. Because of you.
And to CM, I said that it was your tattoos & broken English.
I was clearly mistaken. It was your smiling eyes. LHRA til the end.

Dad, this is my contribution to the family name. You're welcome.

Poppy, your life continues through the smile of your girls.
The extra scoop of ice cream always for you.

To the children. May there come a day when every child can live
with as much joy & peace as they offer to the world.

First Edition November 2023

Written by: Dannielle Levy
Illustrated by: Rebecca Lisotta
Layout/Graphic Design by: Giusy Marrocchella

THE SAD PRINCESS
The search for a happily-ever-after smile

by Dannielle Levy

Illustrated by Rebecca Lisotta

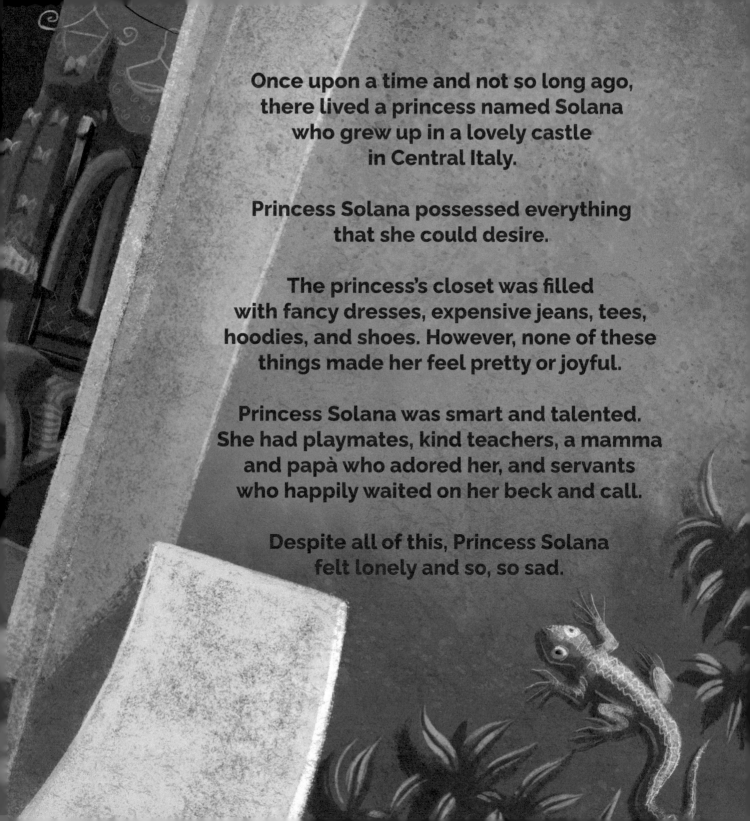

Once upon a time and not so long ago,
there lived a princess named Solana
who grew up in a lovely castle
in Central Italy.

Princess Solana possessed everything
that she could desire.

The princess's closet was filled
with fancy dresses, expensive jeans, tees,
hoodies, and shoes. However, none of these
things made her feel pretty or joyful.

Princess Solana was smart and talented.
She had playmates, kind teachers, a mamma
and papà who adored her, and servants
who happily waited on her beck and call.

Despite all of this, Princess Solana
felt lonely and so, so sad.

You see, one day her smile simply disappeared.
It was as if Princess Solana's heart had been struck
by a magic spell that made everything dark and ugly.

Every day her mamma would say,
*"Good morning my little princess!
Why don't you grant me a beautiful smile today?"*

And, every day
Solana would reply,
"I simply cannot
smile Mammi.
I feel oh so, so sad."

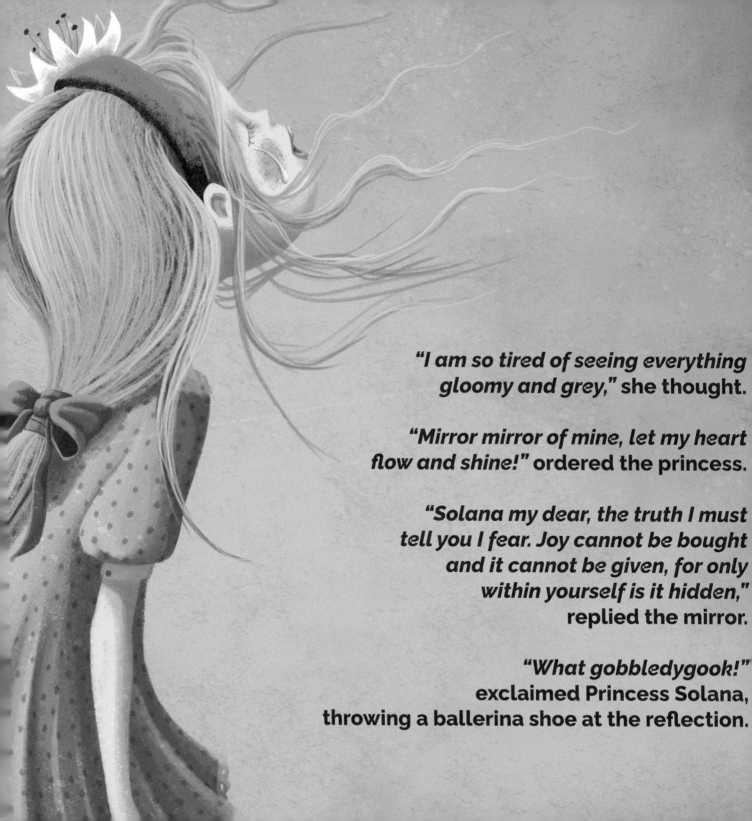

"I am so tired of seeing everything gloomy and grey," she thought.

"Mirror mirror of mine, let my heart flow and shine!" ordered the princess.

"Solana my dear, the truth I must tell you I fear. Joy cannot be bought and it cannot be given, for only within yourself is it hidden," replied the mirror.

"What gobbledygook!" exclaimed Princess Solana, throwing a ballerina shoe at the reflection.

"Call for the most talented painter in all the kingdom," instructed the princess to her servant.

"*Paint me a smile!*" she commanded when
the artist presented himself humbly before her.
And, so he did.

The artisan drew a perfect smile on Princess Solana's pout.

Princess Solana was in sunny spirits as she prepared
for bed that evening. However, when she paused before
the mirror, it was her joyless self that stared back at her.

"*Big yikes!*" cried the princess.
"*I shouldn't have wet my face!*"

"*Keep searching my child and do not get discouraged,
one day a solution will appear along with your invincible
courage,*" her magic mirror tenderly said.

The next morning Princess Solana ordered her servant to call for the funniest comedian in all of Europe.

"Make me smile!" she demanded when the young man presented himself humbly before her.

And so he did.
He entertained and she laughed
'til the wee hours of the night.

At long last, both were simply too tired,
and the princess's eyes said *nighty-night*,
along with her bubbly mood.

The sad princess tried many things while
searching for her happily-ever-after smile.

She rode up, down, and all around on a soaring
roller coaster. At first, she smiled from ear to ear.
But it wasn't long before her head began to spin
and the gleam on her face was gone anew.

She ordered her servant to tickle her.
She tried laughter yoga, salsa dancing,
and clown school. However, her smile
was always destined to fade.

Then one day, Princess Solana overheard
her servants speaking.

*"Why can't our princess be more like the happy
princess?"* one of the servants asked.
*"She is always so joyful and brightens her entire
kingdom with her smile."*

"Who is this happy princess?" thought Solana.
*"And, why is she so joyful and smiley?
I must meet with her and insist that
she reveal her secrets of happiness to me,"*
she whispered to the magic mirror.

*"Go with bravery and an open mind,
and surely the fate of your smile will be
found in a mysterious soul that
is strong and beautiful and kind,"*
replied the mirror.

The following day, Princess Solana began her journey toward the kingdom of the mysteriously happy princess.

When she finally arrived at the castle grounds, Princess Solana couldn't believe her eyes.

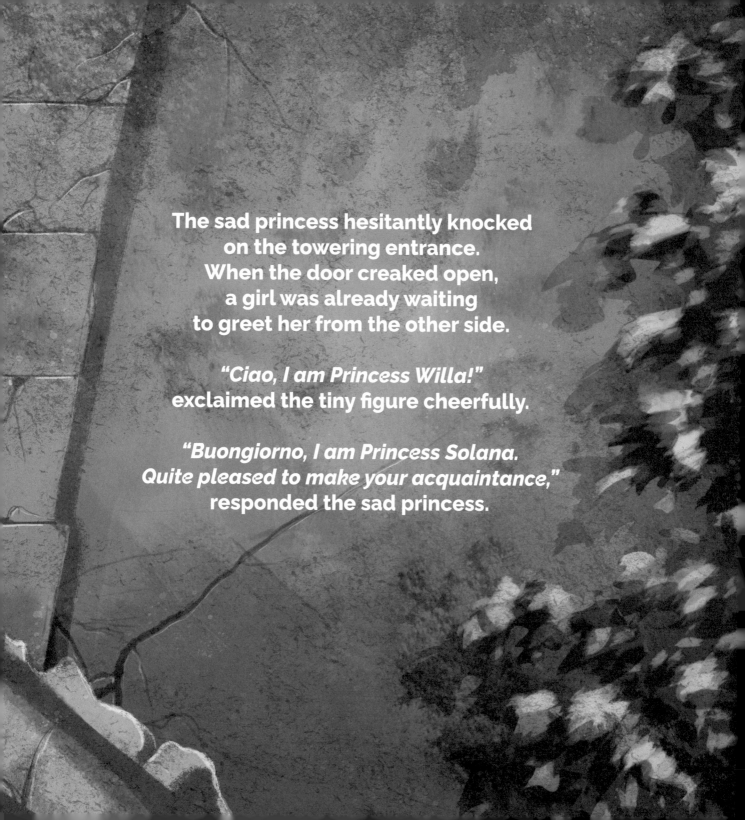

The sad princess hesitantly knocked
on the towering entrance.
When the door creaked open,
a girl was already waiting
to greet her from the other side.

"Ciao, I am Princess Willa!"
exclaimed the tiny figure cheerfully.

"Buongiorno, I am Princess Solana.
Quite pleased to make your acquaintance,"
responded the sad princess.

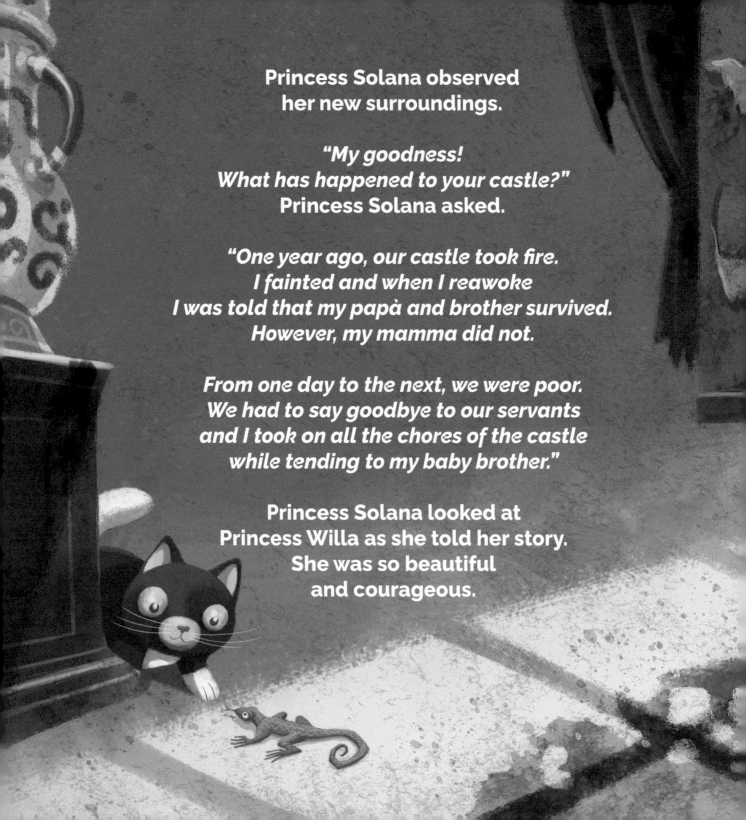

Princess Solana observed
her new surroundings.

*"My goodness!
What has happened to your castle?"*
Princess Solana asked.

*"One year ago, our castle took fire.
I fainted and when I reawoke
I was told that my papà and brother survived.
However, my mamma did not.*

*From one day to the next, we were poor.
We had to say goodbye to our servants
and I took on all the chores of the castle
while tending to my baby brother."*

Princess Solana looked at
Princess Willa as she told her story.
She was so beautiful
and courageous.

"How can you be so happy when you have
lost your mamma and everything else?"
asked Princess Solana.

"After the fire," replied Princess Willa,
"I didn't feel like smiling anymore.
Everything was grey. I kept repeating,
Why did this happen to me?
Then several weeks later,
a fairy spoke to me in my sleep."

"Little princess," said the fairy,
"your mamma was luminous,
and she always met difficulty
with a great, big smile.
She would not want to see you so sad.

You may not feel it yet, but you possess
the strength and graceful beauty
of an enchanting willow tree.
This is why she named you Willa.
Your mamma is with you always.
Your smile, which is so similar to hers,
will remind you that there is so much
to be happy and grateful for.
So, smile my dear."

"When I woke, I felt a golden ball of light
in my heart," continued Princess Willa.
"I knew that it was my mammi.
From that moment, I decided to be brave.
Things immediately started to change.

Solana, perhaps you see all that is destroyed
around me. And, it is so. However, I also see the bees
buzzing around the newly bloomed flowers.
I see that the birds have begun to sing outside
my window again. I see that we are fixing the castle.
I see that our servants have returned
and are now a part of our family."

"So what is your secret to happiness?" **asked Princess Solana still confused.**

"I just decided!" burst out Princess Willa.

"Every day I choose to see all that is beautiful instead of all that has been lost.

I can miss my mammi and feel joyful at the same time," concluded Princess Willa with a great big, beautiful grin.

Princess Solana smiled back at her new friend.

Before saying farewell, the two princesses promised to see each other again soon.

When Princess Solana arrived back at the castle,
she found a note on the kitchen table.

Our dear princess,
We are sorry that we
could not be home to
greet you.
Tomorrow you must
tell us all about
your adventure.

Love you too, too much,
Mammi and Papā

PS: I made the
cherry pie
just for you!

Princess Solana smiled
and after eating
a giant slice of pie,
she went to bed with
a fuzzy feeling in her heart.

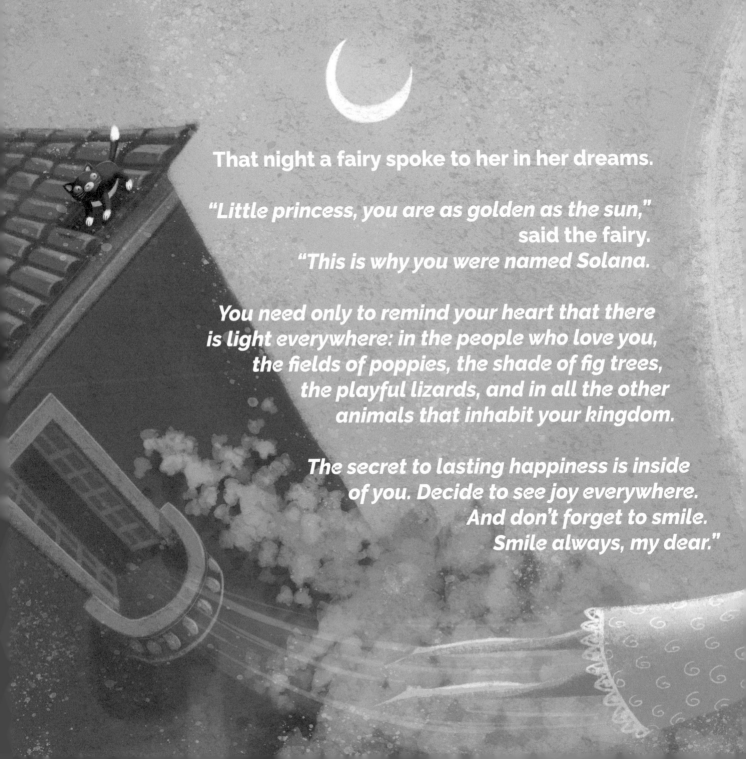

That night a fairy spoke to her in her dreams.

"Little princess, you are as golden as the sun,"
said the fairy.
"This is why you were named Solana.

You need only to remind your heart that there
is light everywhere: in the people who love you,
the fields of poppies, the shade of fig trees,
the playful lizards, and in all the other
animals that inhabit your kingdom.

The secret to lasting happiness is inside
of you. Decide to see joy everywhere.
And don't forget to smile.
Smile always, my dear."

Princess Solana woke up smiling.
Her happiness felt like vanilla
ice cream melting in her tummy.

From then on, when her mamma
came to greet her each morning,
Princess Solana greeted her back
with a smile as bright as
the first peep of sunshine.

Of course, she would still feel sad
sometimes. But Princess Solana
was no longer a sad princess.

She finally discovered how
to always refind her happiness
and her beautiful,
happily-ever-after smile!

THE END.

Here's a little secret:

When I find myself feeling lonely or blue,
I close my eyes and think of
sweet things like popsicles
and the soft whiskers of my kitty FruFru!

And if your mouth has turned upside down,
it is not difficult to turn it back around:

Fill your heart with a big breath while thinking 1,2,3 and 4,
then slowly puff out the silly word 'CHAT-TA-NOO-GA',
and the happy you will appear once more!

CONNECT WITH ME
On the blog www.inspiredwithdanni.com
On FB, IG, Pinterest & YouTube @inspiredwithdanni

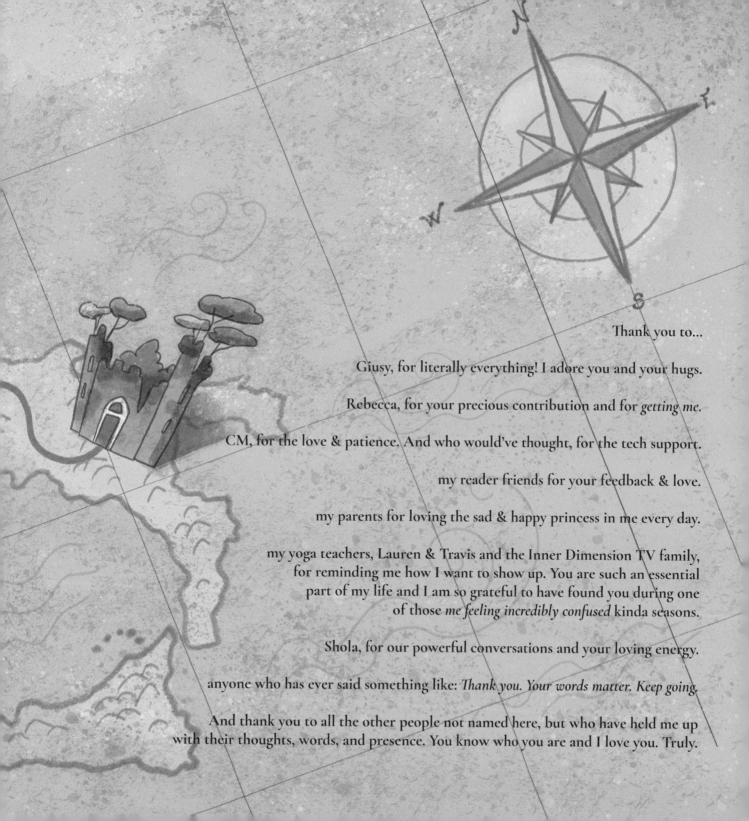

Thank you to...

Giusy, for literally everything! I adore you and your hugs.

Rebecca, for your precious contribution and for *getting me*.

CM, for the love & patience. And who would've thought, for the tech support.

my reader friends for your feedback & love.

my parents for loving the sad & happy princess in me every day.

my yoga teachers, Lauren & Travis and the Inner Dimension TV family,
for reminding me how I want to show up. You are such an essential
part of my life and I am so grateful to have found you during one
of those *me feeling incredibly confused* kinda seasons.

Shola, for our powerful conversations and your loving energy.

anyone who has ever said something like: *Thank you. Your words matter. Keep going.*

And thank you to all the other people not named here, but who have held me up
with their thoughts, words, and presence. You know who you are and I love you. Truly.

Made in the USA
Columbia, SC
28 December 2023

28658521R10020